SANTA ANA PUBLIC LIBRARY

THE Enchanted Umbrella

The ENCHANTED UMBRELLA

STORY BY Odette Meyers

BASED ON A FRENCH FOLKTALE

PICTURES BY Margot Zemach

WITH A SHORT HISTORY OF THE UMBRELLA

GULLIVER BOOKS

HARCOURT BRACE JOVANOVICH

San Diego Austin Orlando

Library of Congress Cataloging-in-Publication Data
Meyers, Odette.
The enchanted umbrella / retold by Odette Meyers : illustrated by Margot Zemach.
p. cm.
"Gulliver books."
Summary: Patou escapes from danger and finds fame and fortune with the aid of a magic umbrella. Includes historical information about umbrellas.
ISBN 0-15-200448-3
[1. Folklore—France. 2. Umbrellas and parasols—Folklore.]
I. Zemach, Margot, ill. II. Title.
PZ8.1.M57Ec 1988
398.2'0944—dc19
[E] 87-30723

Printed in Singapore
First edition
A B C D E

The illustrations in this book were done in watercolor on Crescent illustration board.
The display type was hand-set in Diotima by Central Graphics, San Diego, California.
The text type was set in Trump Mediaeval by Thompson Type, San Diego, California.
Printed and bound by Tien Wah Press, Singapore
Production supervision by Warren Wallerstein and Rebecca Miller
Designed by Joy Chu

A long time ago, there was an old man who made wonderful umbrellas with Patou, his young helper. The old man and Patou worked very hard in the umbrella shop and lived happily together in the rooms above it. The old man had no children of his own and Patou had no family of his own, but the two loved each other like father and son.

The old man had only one relative—a very lazy and selfish nephew who came to visit now and then, but only to sit and eat sweets.

Then the old man became very ill. When he could work no longer, Patou worked twice as hard and cared for him tenderly. The lazy nephew continued to sit and eat sweets.

One day, the old man called his lazy, selfish nephew to his bedside and said, "When I die, take all I have—my money, my house, and all that is in it—and share it equally with Patou who has taken such good care of me in my old age."

"Yes, Uncle," promised the nephew.

But, as soon as his uncle died, the nephew said to Patou, "Now my uncle's money, his house, and all that is in it belong to me alone. Go away!" And he pushed Patou out of the house.

Patou was very sad. It was raining heavily, so he huddled close to the door. The selfish nephew opened a window and shoved an old ragged umbrella at him, saying, "My uncle has left you this. Now go away!"

Patou took the umbrella. He was very glad to have something that had belonged to the old man, and the umbrella would protect him from the rain.

He had nowhere to go, so he walked aimlessly, holding his umbrella above his head like a traveling roof.

Patou wandered into a forest, where he was attacked by thieves. One of the thieves tried to grab his umbrella from him, but Patou clung tightly to the handle. To their surprise, the boy and the thief rose in the air at a frightening speed.

Patou was afraid he would lose his grip, but the umbrella handle held him fast. Not so the thief, who was shaken off and dropped into the treetops.

Sailing through the air, Patou gazed happily down at the countryside. Far below, he saw a richly dressed couple strolling in a beautiful garden. Suddenly, he spotted a tiger about to pounce on them.

He gave his umbrella a gentle pull, and at once it swooped down into the garden. "Quick, a tiger!" Patou cried as he grabbed the couple. Immediately, the umbrella rose swiftly into the air, carrying them to safety.

Patou and the umbrella took the couple right to the front door of their grand mansion.

"Won't you come in?" the rich man asked as he eyed the umbrella greedily.

"Yes, I will. Thank you very much," said Patou as he closed his umbrella carefully.

Inside, they all sat down to a festive meal. The rich man offered Patou a great deal of money for his umbrella. But Patou refused politely, saying, "No thank you, sir. This umbrella was a very special gift, and I would not part with it for anything in the world."

The rich man still wanted the umbrella for himself, and he had an idea. He ordered his servant to bring a very strong wine for Patou, who drank it and promptly fell sound asleep.

While Patou was sleeping, the rich man took the umbrella. Eager to try out its magic, he opened it inside the house. At once the umbrella yanked him out the door and whisked him up into the air.

As they flew over a river, the umbrella closed abruptly and dropped into the water with the frightened man still clinging to the handle.

Some fishermen who happened to be nearby pulled the rich man from the river and carried him to his house.

Patou, awakened by all the commotion, looked for his umbrella, but could not find it. "Thief! Thief!" he cried.

The rich man heard Patou's cries. Soaking wet and furious, he shouted, "Throw that boy in the river!" His cruel servants obeyed him.

Patou struggled and kept yelling, "Thief! Thief!" but the servants held him fast. From the steepest rock by the river's edge, they flung the screaming boy headfirst into the icy water.

Patou sank, then rose to the surface. He sank again, but managed to rise once more. Just as he was about to sink for the third time, he saw his umbrella, floating upside-down at his side.

With great difficulty, he clambered into the umbrella. Together Patou and his umbrella sailed down the river, all the way to the ocean, through calm waters and stormy waters . . .

After many days, Patou landed on a faraway shore. He was delighted to be back on land. He turned his umbrella right side up, and it joyfully carried him high above a crowd of astonished people who had never seen an umbrella before.

"Long, long ago," said one very old man, "kings had umbrellas!"

So, when Patou landed among the people, they crowned him their king. They gave him a fine, cheerful house with a beautiful flower garden. Once again, Patou had a home. He was very happy.

King Patou made a speech: "Dear people, I thank you for the fine house and the beautiful garden. And I thank you for the crown; I will wear it always. And now, as your king, I will make my first law. Let each one, young and old, have an umbrella. But do understand that only *my* umbrella can fly. It belonged to an old umbrella maker who once gave me a loving home and a useful trade."

Since only King Patou knew how to make umbrellas, he set up a shop in his fine house. He hired many helpers. And, with his crown on his head and the royal umbrella close by, he made umbrellas for all the people of his kingdom.

Now the old ragged umbrella had nothing to do but protect King Patou from the rain. Once in a while, it got restless and would suddenly pull him up into the air. Sometimes when he felt like it . . . and sometimes when he didn't .

. . . And more about umbrellas

(A SHORT HISTORY)

Long, long ago, only kings and emperors, sultans, and other rulers were allowed to own an umbrella. It was a sign of power.

Mongolian Emperor

Then . . .
the rulers began to give
umbrellas to some of their
friends, and relatives, and their
favorite guests.

Burma

Africa

Siam

Italy

wedding in India

But . . .
in time, so many people admired umbrellas and wished to have them that there came to be two kinds: very fancy ones for royal families and ceremonial occasions; and simpler, more practical ones for everyday use by ordinary people.

umbrella seller - England

Carnival in New Orleans

marketplace - Japan

Luckily for us, today everyone who wants an umbrella can have one: a fancy one or a simple one . . . .

Some people think that . . .

if you open your umbrella inside a house, it will bring you bad luck . . .

But . . .

all you have to do is close the umbrella and walk backwards through the front door . . .

. . . and the bad luck is undone!